TRIO +1

by
Jordan Campbell, Rico McCard,
and Brandon Smith

Illustrated by Lucia Liu

Reach Education, Inc. | Washington, DC

Reach: Books by Teens
Published by
Reach Education, Inc.
www.reachincorporated.org

Copyright © 2013 Reach Education, Inc.

ISBN: 0615884709
ISBN-13: 978-0615884707

DEDICATION

To anyone who ever thought they didn't fit in.

Look at those three.

Rodney with his book bag.
Who knows how many good grades he has.

Chase and his paintings.
He wins every art contest.

Rico, star of the basketball team.
I knew I should've tried out.

And then there's me. Big Bobby.
Head of the newspaper at Reach Middle School.

Do I win everything?
No.
Clearly not.
But I do so much.

I write articles for the paper.
I take good pictures.

And do I get any recognition?
Not at all.

One day soon, I'll end their
happy trio.
And I'll have all the
recognition I want.

One day, I'm reading different stories submitted by other students, and I come across one that says, "Coolest Kid."

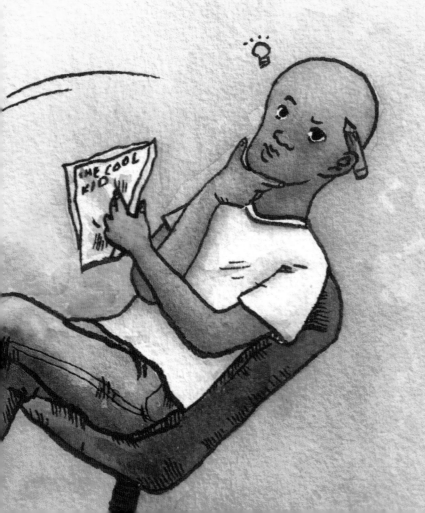

So I think to myself, *I should create a competition between Rico, Rodney, and Chase to see who is the coolest kid.*

Maybe then, they won't be friends.

I'm walking down the hallway, and I overhear Rico, Rodney, and Chase say they are the best of friends. I remember a time when we were all best friends. Back when we used to hang out as elementary kids. Back before they started getting all the awards.

Later on in the lunchroom, I ask them if they've seen the newspaper.

They give me a confused look and say, "What are you talking about?"

"You know, in the paper. You three guys are competing against each other to see who is the coolest kid," I say.

"Oh for real? I had five people come up to me to say congratulations and good luck. I was wondering what that was about," Rodney says.

Then Chase says, "Yeah, me too. I had like four people come up to me and say good luck with the contest. That's what they were talking about!"

He sighs. "But I didn't sign up for anything."

"Did y'all sign up for anything?" Rodney asks.

The two other boys shake their heads.

"I didn't even know about it," Chase says.

I have to think fast on my feet, so I quickly say, "You guys didn't have to sign up. The 6th graders voted."

Of course this is a lie. I picked their names myself.

"Really? That's cool," Rico exclaims, looking proud.

"What are you talking about? You're really going through with this?" Chase asks.

"We're best friends, so why are we competing against each other?" Rodney asks, with a confused look on his face.

"I'm just letting you guys know what's going on in the school," I say. "So I'm gonna go back to the newspaper office."

As I watch them leave to go to class, I can tell Rico's feelin' to do the competition. I'm happy. Maybe my plan will work after all.

I see Rico walking to class, so I run up and talk to him.

"You should really look forward to doing this competition," I say.

"Well I was just talking about it with the guys in the lunchroom. We were saying that it wasn't really a good idea," Rico says with hesitation.

Uh oh. I have to think quickly about what will make Rico want to join.

"But wouldn't you like to win MVP again? If you participate this will give you more votes," I say.

This is Rico's third year being nominated for MVP, and I know there is a school record at stake.

"Yeah, if I win, I would be the first middle schooler ever to win three years in a row," Rico says. He looks skeptical, but interested.

"Exactly!" I say. "Your coach already contacted the newspaper to find out when the Coolest Kid results would be announced."

I am lying fast and furious, but I need Rico to join if my plan is going to have a chance.

Rico looks at the trophies lining the hallway. There is an empty space for this year's MVP.

"Yeah, OK," Rico says. "I'm in."

Nice. I have Rico doing the contest. Now my plan is to get Rodney in as well.

"See you Wednesday at the first competition," I say.

It's the next day and I see Rodney at breakfast by himself, so I go over and talk to him.

"Rodney, you know that Rico is going to be in the competition to beat you."

"Why would he do that?" Rodney asks. "He's my best friend."

"Because he cares more about getting MVP than your friendship," I say.

This is sure to make Rodney not trust Rico, breaking up their friendship.

Rodney looks hurt. "Oh for real? Well I guess I'll be in the competition, too." He shrugs.

This is great. My plan is really going well so far.

Now I just need to get Chase.

Two periods later, it's lunchtime and I see Chase headed to the lunchroom. When we get there, Rodney and Rico are sitting at separate tables.

Chase turns to me and says, "What's up with these guys? Why are they sitting at separate tables?"

"Oh you haven't heard?" I say slyly.

"Haven't heard what?" Chase asks.

"They are entering the Coolest Kid Competition," I say.

Chase shakes his head. "Really, though? They're going to enter the competition without even telling me? I thought we were friends. Scratch that, I thought we were *best* friends. But I guess not, doing things like that. So just let me know when and where. I'll be there."

I turn my back towards Chase and smile.

"The first event is tomorrow at lunch. See you then."

That night, I am too excited to go to sleep.

Tomorrow I see my plan working: those three won't be friends anymore, and more importantly, people will notice what I do.

I won't be invisible.

The next day, it is lunchtime, the big day.
The Coolest Kid Competition.

You can hear the kids chanting as Rico, Rodney, and Chase
step into the lunchroom, all going to their separate crowds.

I had decided that the first competition would be basketball.

We all make our way to the gym. The balls are already set up, three racks around the hoop.

Rico goes first and he makes all of his shots.

His crowd goes wild.

Rodney scores two and Chase
ends up scoring one.

Rico wins the first competition.

He seems happy he won, smiling
at his fans, but as soon as everyone
looks away, he's frowning.

As they head to the art room, I overhear Chase and Rodney say that they aren't as interested in the contest as Rico is.

I get a little closer.

"I knew Bobby shouldn't have convinced me to get into this game." Chase sighs.

"Yeah, he convinced me, too," Rodney says. "I wonder if he convinced Rico?"

I'm starting to feel like my master plan is falling apart.

I try to hurry the crowd to the next event before Chase and Rodney have a chance to talk to Rico.

Once I get to the art room, it seems like they're all still against each other. I'm not too late.

The second competition is for them to draw a tree that is losing its leaves. Sort of like the cover of *The Giving Tree*.

Chase wins it by a long shot. Rodney gets second. Rico gets third.

Chase is excited and happy he won, but Rico and Rodney look angrily over at Chase. We head to the last event.

The last event is in Ms. Jusna's room. This event is to test knowledge. Ms. Jusna asks them to solve a math problem with the quadratic formula and to analyze a poem.

This time, of course, Rodney wins with straight A's. Rico and Chase don't get any of the questions right.

Rodney wins the whole competition, based off of the points from the previous events.

Just as I had imagined, Chase and Rico have their heads down.

All of a sudden, Chase storms out of the room. Rico follows with a disgusted look toward Rodney. Rodney looks disappointed in himself.

I happily rejoice inside. I have finally ruined the trio.

So I go upstairs to my office to write the last few sentences in the newspaper about the event.

A few minutes later, Chase, Rico, and Rodney storm into my office.

"We know what you are doing. This whole thing was fake!" they scream at the exact same time.

"You lied to me about MVP," Rico says. "I asked Coach, and he said he didn't even know about the Coolest Kid Competition. You were using me."

"I have no idea what you're talking about," I say coolly, shuffling papers on my desk.

I look over to my pad that had my whole plan on it. At the top it says: "Coolest Kid Competition." Then it lists ways to break up the trio.

Chase catches a glimpse and exclaims, "Right there!"

"Bobby, why did you do this?" Rodney asks.

I look down at the desk. I don't want to look at them when I say this.

"I did it because all of y'all were getting respect at school from the other students, and I basically did all the work, and never got credit for it. Nobody ever noticed me."

Rico sighs. Chase nods his head.

"You don't have to ruin friendships to get attention. We've always been friends," Rodney says.

"If you didn't feel like you were getting noticed as much, you could've just said something," Chase says.

"Friends? I didn't think we were friends," I say, surprised.

"Yeah, you've always been our friend. We wondered why you avoided us once we got to middle school."

I look at their confused faces and think about these past couple of years.

Was it them that stopped hanging out with me, or was it me that stopped hanging out with them?

When I think about it, maybe it was the other way around.

There were times that Rico asked if we could play basketball, but I said no for fear of looking bad compared to Rico's skills. Rodney and Chase asked to play games or study. I always refused.

"Chase, Rodney, Rico, I apologize for setting you guys up in this Coolest Kid Competition. I just wanted to end what was so happy for you. I didn't know that we were friends like that. I'll do anything to make it up."

The guys all look at each other, deciding.

"So why don't you write a story, and give yourself some recognition too?" Rodney asks.

The next day my story comes out on the front page.

It's the best story
I've written.

THE END

Acknowledgments

In July 2013, fifteen students embarked on an exciting journey. Tasked with creating original children's books, these young people brainstormed ideas, generated potential plots, wrote, revised, and provided critiques. In the end, four amazing books were created, showing again what teenagers can do when their potential is unleashed with purpose. Our fifteen authors have our immense gratitude and respect: Joshua, Jordan, Rashaan, Za'Metria, Marc, Sasha, Dana, Rico, Sejal, Angelo, Sean, Brandon, DaQuan, Kyare, and Zorita.

We also appreciate the leadership provided by our instructional leaders: Kaitlyn Denzler, Andrea Mirviss, and Brian Ovalles. Jusna Perrin, in addition to leading a team of teen writers, steered our summer program ship, seemingly with ease.

We also owe great thanks to our talented illustrators, Lucia Liu and Mira Ko, whose beautiful drawings brought these stories to life. And, most of all, we thank our dedicated and inspiring writing coach, Kathy Crutcher, who led our teens from the excitement of brainstorming through the hard work of revision to make these stories the best they can be.

Once the books were finished, publication costs could have made it difficult to share these stories with the world, so we appreciate the financial support provided by the New York Avenue Presbyterian Church, the Carr Family, the Denzler Family, Helen Runnells DuBois, the Hollowell Family, the Mirviss Family, and Cheryl Zabinski.

Most of all, we thank those of you who have purchased the books. We hope the smiles created as you read match those expressed as we wrote.

About the Authors

Jordan Campbell was born and raised in SE DC and is a junior at Eastern Senior High School. He was born into an artistic family, always inspiring him to be creative, but he's not exactly sure how. In the meantime, he's looking at different careers to pursue. You can always find Jordan with his headphones on and listening to music.

Rico McCard was born in Washington, DC on May 15th, 1997. He is a sophomore at Eastern Senior High School. He likes playing basketball, making people laugh, and going out. And he loves his family. He plans on being a psychologist after attending the University of Maryland, College Park.

Brandon Smith is 17 years old and a senior at Perry Street Prep Public Charter School in NE DC. He's into tutoring kids and helping younger children read. In pursuing this love, he wanted to write this book with two of his colleagues. He's looking forward to writing more books.

About the Illustrator

Lucia Liu is a sophomore at VCUarts, majoring in Painting & Printmaking and minoring in Creative Entrepreneurship. She has experience in fine art, art education, studio assisting, and illustration. In addition to art, she loves playing music and has participated in musical ensembles as a violinist for nearly ten years. More of her work can be found at lucialiu.wix.com/artportfolio.

About the Story Coach

Kathy Crutcher has mentored young writers since 2003 and is passionate about empowering others to tell their stories. After coaching the teen tutors of Reach Incorporated to write their first four books in 2013, she was inspired to found Shout Mouse Press, a writing program and publishing house for unheard voices. To learn more, visit www.shoutmousepress.org.

About Reach Incorporated

Reach Incorporated develops confident grade-level readers and capable leaders by training teens to teach, creating academic benefit for all involved.

Founded in 2009, Reach recruits entering 9th grade students to be elementary school tutors. Elementary school students average 1.5 grade levels of reading growth per year of participation. This growth – equal to that created by highly effective teachers – is created by high school students who average more than two grade levels of growth per year of program participation.

Reach creates readers. Reach creates leaders. And, by lifting two populations through a uniquely structured relationship, Reach is effectively attacking Washington DC's literacy crisis.

During the summer of 2013, Reach launched a new program to build on school-year gains made by program tutors. As part of this program, teens partnered with professional writers and illustrators to create original children's stories. These stories, written entirely by our teens, provide our young people with the opportunity to share their talents and creativity with a wider audience.

By purchasing our books, you support student-led, community-driven efforts to improve educational outcomes in the District of Columbia.

Learn more at www.reachincorporated.org.

Made in the USA
Charleston, SC
29 May 2015